Murder in Windy Hollow
A Beth Sanders Cozy Mystery

Windy Hollow Mysteries

Iris Kingsley

PUBLISHING

Introduction

Welcome to Windy Hollow, where secrets simmer and murder is on the menu.

After losing both her mother and husband in the span of three years, Beth trades a sterile food styling career in Atlanta for the cozy chaos of reopening her late mother's beloved bakery. With a loyal corgi named Snickers, a pantry full of memories, and a town steeped in cinnamon and nostalgia, she's ready to rebuild her life—one lemon bar at a time.

But when a famed local historian drops dead during a book signing and a mysterious fire blazes behind the inn, Beth finds herself up to her elbows in more than just batter.

As whispers of a century-old vault and forged family legacies swirl through the village, Beth—armed with nothing but intuition, a teacup-shaped cookie cutter, and her quirky best friend Penny—follows a trail of half-baked secrets that lead right to Windy Hollow's most influential family.

Now, with anonymous warnings slipping under her welcome mat, and her social media suddenly lighting up thanks to a viral Snickers video, Beth must decide how far she's willing to go for the truth.

Because in Windy Hollow, secrets rise faster than sourdough, and someone's been tampering with the recipe.

Warm, witty, and sprinkled with suspense, **Murder in Windy Hollow** is the first in a charming cozy mystery series where every clue is baked with love, and solving a murder might just be the secret ingredient to finding home again.

Contents

Chapter 1
Preheating the Oven

"No, Snickers!! You menace! Come here right now!"

Beth Sanders stood in the center of her bakery, elbow-deep in cinnamon roll dough, with a streak of flour across her cheek and a determined glint in her hazel eyes. At thirty-five, with practical brown hair tucked behind one ear and a dusting of freckles across her nose, Beth wore her favorite navy apron with "Whisk Me Away" embroidered across the chest. Her sleeves were rolled to the elbow, her boots dusted in flour, and her heart full of nerves and hope.

She leapt toward the counter just as her corgi launched himself out of a torn flour sack like a furry missile, trailing a comet tail of white powder. The cinnamon-and-cream corgi, stout with short legs and comically oversized ears, darted beneath a table and left behind a trail of floury paw prints.

"I swear, you're a walking powdered doughnut," Beth muttered with a smirk, grabbing a dishtowel and skidding across the floor in pursuit.

Snickers let out a playful bark and wiggled his white-dusted rear in triumph.

Her smartwatch buzzed as she cornered him. Are you starting a workout? it asked cheerfully. "Only if chasing a powdered doughnut dog counts," she muttered, dismissing the alert. She'd regret not logging it later—Penny and Manny were already trash-talking over this week's leaderboard.

"You are not getting a treat! Quit looking at me like that," she said.

It was early spring in Windy Hollow, the kind where blossoms flirt with the breeze and the air carries the scent of fresh grass and possibility. Outside the shop windows, the world was in bloom. Dogwoods stretched their arms in pinks and whites while the breeze carried the scent of wet earth and renewal. Inside the bakery, however, the air was thick with the smell of brown sugar, rising yeast, and a flour-covered tornado.

Finally, Beth scooped up her rebellious pup. Both were now dusted in flour like absurd mimes caught mid-performance. She cradled him in her arms and chuckled. "If I ever lose this bakery, we'll start a street act, you and me. Evelyn would've had a fit."

She turned slowly to take in the space she'd poured every ounce of energy into for the past six months.

Just days before signing the lease, she'd stood alone in the center of the empty shop with her keys and a heart full of doubts. She had stared at the scuffed wood floors and sun-faded walls and asked aloud if she was crazy. If chasing this dream alone—without Graham, without Evelyn—was a beautiful tribute or a desperate gamble. But then she'd heard her mom's voice in her head, clear as sunrise: "Comfort food doesn't fix everything, but it sure makes it easier to talk about." And she'd laughed. Then cried. Then picked up a paintbrush.

Because if there was ever a legacy worth building, this was it.

Wooden tables, rustic with character. Fresh daffodils in mason jars. Pale green walls and golden sconces casting a warm light across honey-toned floors. The counter gleamed, topped with glass jars filled with lemon drops and cinnamon sticks. Her mom's favorite apron hung near the oven, just as it had in their old kitchen.

"You'd love this place, Mom," Beth whispered. "You really would."

When Evelyn passed, Beth had been working at a food styling company in Atlanta—deadlines and stylized plating, all sterile perfection. The grief cracked her open. She took a leave of absence and never returned.

Three years before that, Graham's death had left her drifting. Losing her mother had set her searching. Windy Hollow had always been home—hers as much as Evelyn's.

She and her mom had lived here until Beth left for culinary school in Charleston, chasing experience but always carrying the flavors of home. She remembered standing beside her mother in their yellow farmhouse kitchen. The oven door squeaked, and the windows fogged with cinnamon-scented steam. Evelyn baked for everyone—the hospital staff, church potlucks, the heartbroken neighbor two doors down.

Beth helped, sometimes more enthusiastically than skillfully—especially when she doubled the vanilla or sneakily added sugar.

She still remembered Evelyn's voice as she passed over a pie to a neighbor: "We don't just bake to feed bellies, sweetheart. We bake to feed hearts."

That line had stayed with her.

Now, after all this time, she was the one baking. Not in the same creaky kitchen—but in a space Evelyn would've adored. A dream space. A real bakery.

Windy Hollow didn't just hold her childhood. It held everything. Her roots. Her memories. Her next chapter. Evelyn would have been over the moon to see Beth turn their family legacy into something that could welcome the whole town in off the street and send them home a little warmer than they came.

She had followed those memories here.

She had poured her mother's recipes into the bones of the bakery. Not because she was chasing the past— well, maybe a little—but because it felt like the right way to build something new.

And now, she was opening in less than a week.

Scratching Snickers absently now, she turned back toward the counter where the hand-painted sign leaned against the wall. 'Sweet Traditions.'

Beth frowned. "Still not the right name."

Mom had a saying: "If your name doesn't taste good on the tongue, you don't serve it with tea."

Beth bit her lip. The bakery needed something more... Evelyn. Something that wrapped legacy and lemon bars into one warm phrase.

The bell above the door jingled.

"Do I smell impending chaos or just your usual flour facial?"

Beth turned, still holding the snow-dusted dog, to see Penelope Whittaker—Penny to her closest friends—standing in the doorway. Her auburn curls spilled from beneath a knitted beret, and she held two takeaway coffees and a bright, amused expression.

"Bit of both," Beth sighed, depositing Snickers on a stool. "He's decided flour is the new dog bed."

"Is that mime work or modern art?"

"I was thinking interpretive dance."

"Performance piece: 'The Ghost of Bakeries Past.'"

Beth chuckled and took the coffee. "You're early."

"You're covered in flour. We all have our crosses."

Snickers gave a half-hearted sneeze and looked entirely unrepentant.

Penny reached down and scratched his head. "He needs a cape. Maybe a beret."

"Don't give him ideas. He already has a sweater collection that rivals mine."

"So, how's my favorite mildly caffeinated baker this morning?"

"Oh, you know. Terrified. Excited. Flour-covered. The usual."

"Sounds like progress."

Beth took a long sip of coffee and leaned against the counter. "I still haven't decided on a name."

"Sweet Traditions? Hmm." Penny squinted. "It's nice. Polished. But... it doesn't sing. Doesn't say Beth Sanders lives here."

"Exactly," Beth agreed. "I want it to feel like Mom and I are still baking together. That every scone has a story."

"You'll find the name. You're building something real here."

Beth nodded, eyes scanning the room again. Penny was right. This wasn't just a bakery. It was a warm corner of the world stitched together with sugar and memories.

Snickers let out a loud yawn and sprawled across the stool as if exhausted by the flour incident.

"That's no help at all," Beth told him. "But I suppose your theatrical contribution counts."

The bell jingled again.

"Speaking of chaos," Penny whispered.

Manny Piccott strolled in, brushing wind from his dark curls and what looked suspiciously like hay from his shoulders. His eyes scanned the room, quick and observant, the hint of a crease between his brows smoothing only once he saw everyone safe and laughing.

"And what is happening here? Is this dog committing kitchen crimes?"

"Don't encourage him, Officer," Beth said, tossing a dish towel over Snickers' head.

"He's a rogue, that's for sure," Manny replied. "Big day. Opening treats and literary legends."

"You'd think royalty was visiting," Penny said. "Between the banner at the inn and Mrs. Pettigrew's new hat, you'd think Simon Caldwell was announcing his candidacy for mayor."

"He might uncover some scandal that leads to a mayoral resignation," Manny added. "I heard he exposed a whole town's fake ancestry records in Vermont. They retaliated with pies."

"What flavor?" Beth asked.

"Blueberry, I think. Or outrage."

Beth chuckled, her eyes softening. These people were her family now. Her support system. Her tribe. Mom would have liked them all—especially Penny and Manny. Especially Penny, who had once driven an hour to help Beth test croissant laminations.

"What's he like?" she asked. "Simon, I mean."

"Sharp. Clever. Not much for smiling," Penny said. "He stopped in yesterday to confirm details. Didn't even pretend to look charmed."

"Maybe he saves it for his readers," Manny offered. "Or maybe Windy Hollow's not edgy enough."

"Oh, just wait until he meets Hilda Pettigrew," Penny said. "She told me she has fire cider steeped in secrets."

Beth wiped her hands. "I just hope the shop can keep up once Simon makes us famous."

"You'll be swamped," Penny said.

"We might finally get that stop sign on Elm," Manny added.

The door opened again, quietly this time.

Jack Tilley entered. Everything about him was polished, from his navy coat to his salt-and-pepper beard. He had a way of walking like the floor owed him rent.

"Ladies. Officer Piccott," he greeted with a politician's smile.

"Beth's nearly ready," Penny said. "Just waiting on a sign from the pastry gods."

"Caldwell's arrival seems to have stirred quite the excitement," Jack said, eyeing the counter. "His stories often shape legacies. I expect he'll find ours... notable."

Beth met his gaze. It was polite but probing.

He continued. "I trust Mr. Caldwell's arrival will put Windy Hollow where it belongs—on the map. The Tilley family has always been a pillar of this town's history."

Beth offered a polite smile. Jack Tilley and humility had never shared the same coffee. There was always something in the way he spoke—smooth as glass, but a little too polished, a little too aware of the effect he had on a room. Not Beth's cup of tea, that was for sure.

Manny shifted. Penny raised a brow.

"Well," Jack said, the corners of his mouth tight, "I look forward to reading about it."

He left with a nod, the scent of expensive cologne lingering.

"Why do I always feel like he should be twirling a mustache?" Penny asked.

"Because if he had one, he would," Manny muttered.

Beth stared at the door long after Jack disappeared. There was pride in his voice, whether for the town or his family namesake it was difficult to tell. Jack Tilley was the president of the Windy Hollow Historical Society.

Membership: one, it seemed.

By late afternoon, the apricot-glazed tarts were cooling by the window ledge. Beth wiped down the counter for the fifth time, glancing out at the golden light dipping behind the treetops.

Snickers snored softly on the stool.

"Almost showtime," Beth whispered. "We've got this, Mom."

Then she heard it.

A crack in the calm. Shouting.

Then—smoke.

Black, thick, curling over the treetops behind the Windy Hollow Inn.

She raced outside, apron flying. Snickers barked and bolted after her.

"Fire! At the workshed!"

"Get water! Buckets!"

Beth grabbed a pail, joining the human chain. Flames licked the sky. The shed groaned.

It didn't burn like old wood. It burned fast. Fierce. Like it had help.

As the smoke cleared and the shed collapsed inward, Beth sniffed. Chemicals. Not just wood.

"It caught fast," Elliott said, breathless. "Like it was waiting."

Beth didn't answer. She was too focused on the acrid tang in the air—sharp, unnatural. Her eyes watered, not just from smoke, but from the surge of dread tightening in her chest.

Shouts echoed. Someone tripped. Another villager ran past carrying a dripping garden hose. The bucket in Beth's hands felt heavier with every pass.

She paused, sweat clinging to her brow, and stared into the curling smoke. This wasn't a random blaze. This was purposeful. Precise.

Snickers barked again, more insistently this time, his paws dancing nervously against the dirt.

Beth squinted into the smoldering remains, her heart hammering as a single, horrible thought crept forward: What if this wasn't just a fire? What if this was a message?

Elliott was standing nearby, hands on his hips, clearly upset and confused. The crowd began to thin, the heat dissipating, but the heaviness in Beth's chest lingered.

Manny took out his notepad, lips pressed into a grim line as he began questioning Elliott.

The warmth of the day soured. And unease settled like ash.

Something in Windy Hollow wasn't right.

And it was only just beginning.

Chapter 2
Cracks in the Crust

Windy Hollow practically hummed with excitement. The early morning sun glinted off cobblestone paths as neighbors bustled about in anticipation of Simon Caldwell's book signing at Pages & Stories. Bunting fluttered from lamp posts and chalkboard signs announced the event with loops of celebratory script. The village's air of quiet charm had been replaced, at least for the day, with a crackling sense of occasion.

Beth Sanders balanced four pastel pastry boxes as she nudged open the door to Penny's bookstore with her shoulder. The familiar chime greeted her, followed closely by the earthy aroma of old books and brewing herbal tea. A moment later, Snickers trotted in behind her, tail wagging, a ribbon tied around his collar. He seemed to know today was special.

"You're a vision," Penny said, rushing over. Her usual beret had been swapped for a headband adorned with a tiny, glittery quill. She looked like the hostess of a very literary tea party.

Beth grinned. "Complimenting me or the goods?"

"Both. But mostly the pastries."

Beth set the boxes on the event table, opening them to reveal an array of scones, tarts, lavender shortbread, and cinnamon twists. Each treat was arranged like a work of art.

"These are going to steal the show. You're going to be famous before Simon even cracks open his book." Penny took a buttertart.

"Let's not overshadow the literary star," Beth replied. "We can't have the poor man upstaged by lemon drizzle."

The event room was cozy but bustling, its usual quiet reading corners transformed into an elegant space with tidy rows of chairs, a small podium, and linen-covered tables adorned with fresh bouquets. Penny had added a touch of whimsy with hand-lettered bookmarks that read "Every Village Has a Story."

By mid-morning, the room was full. Villagers filled the chairs, some clutching well-worn copies of Simon's previous books, others whispering excitedly about what he might reveal in this one.

Beth moved around the room, tray in hand, offering pastries. Her hazel eyes swept over familiar faces: Mrs. Pettigrew in a peacock-blue scarf, the mayor's assistant nervously chewing her lip, Elliott Yates standing stiffly near the back with arms crossed, and Millie Carr from the Historical Preservation Guild adjusting her pince-nez while scanning the crowd for any media presence.

The townsfolk had come out in full force. Roger Tims from the post office chatted animatedly with Greta Moffat, the florist, about how he once delivered a letter to Simon Caldwell years ago, which might've "inspired an entire chapter." Greta, meanwhile, was more interested in whether her bouquet arrangements would end up in any promotional photos.

"Apricot tart?" Beth offered to Mrs. Pettigrew.

"If you twist my arm," the older woman said. "Do you think he'll talk about the Stonehurst scandal? I always said they were too well-dressed for honesty."

"If he does, I hope he includes the part where Hiram Stonehurst tried to bribe the choir director," muttered Carl Jenks from the front row, who'd brought his ancient bulldog snoring quietly under his seat.

Beth smiled politely but said nothing. She noticed the whispers—speculation and stories swirling like whipped cream. That was the thing about Windy Hollow: under its postcard charm, stories brewed like strong tea.

The door opened, and a hush rippled through the room. Simon Caldwell had arrived.

Simon entered with the calm assurance of someone used to commanding a room—tall, lean, and sharply dressed in a tailored charcoal blazer. His glasses sat perfectly on the bridge of his nose, his salt-and-pepper hair slightly tousled as though the wind obeyed him, not the other way around.

"Welcome, everyone," Penny said, stepping up to the podium. "Thank you for joining us for what promises to be a delightful—and possibly eye-opening—discussion. We're thrilled to welcome celebrated author Simon Caldwell."

Polite applause followed.

Simon offered a brief nod. "It's a pleasure to be in Windy Hollow. Your village has more stories hidden beneath its cobblestones than most cities twice its size."

There were a few chuckles, a few proud smiles. Charlie Lane from the village council thumped his cane in agreement, his cane tapping along in approval like a gavel.

Beth moved toward the back, handing Penny a cup of tea and taking a seat with Snickers at her feet. She could feel the tension beginning to hum beneath the surface, like the moment before a kettle whistles.

Simon launched into his talk, weaving tales from his latest book, "Beneath the Surface: Secrets of Windy Hollow's Foundations." His voice was smooth, practiced, but not without warmth, like the kind of professor who knew just how to enchant a lecture hall. He moved through stories like a seasoned performer, drawing gasps and laughter at just the right moments. He recounted local legends about lost love letters discovered in the library walls, mysterious initials carved into the town's oldest oak, and the scandalous tale of a mayor who once faked a broken leg to avoid jury duty.

He spoke not just of Windy Hollow's charm, but of its layered complexity. "This village," he said, gesturing lightly to the audience, "is like a beautiful old book. Its spine is cracked, its margins scribbled with notes, and its pages worn soft from hands that turned them too many times to count."

He paused, then added with measured clarity, "What fascinates me most is not just what people choose to remember—but what they choose to forget."

That line landed like a dropped pin in a silent room. Heads tilted. Breaths caught.

The crowd was silent—reflective. Beth, standing at the back, felt the hairs rise on her arms. That wasn't just eloquence—it was a quiet warning, wrapped in story. A gentle nudge toward the uncomfortable. A reminder that even the sweetest places have shadows if you dig deep enough.

The room stilled.

Beth noticed Elliott Yates shift in his seat, jaw tightening. She recalled Penny mentioning Simon had been less than pleased with his stay at the inn. Something about a draft and an overdone omelet.

"Sometimes," Simon continued, "even the most charming places harbor ghosts. And I don't mean the bedsheet kind."

Uneasy laughter followed. Elliott muttered something and walked toward the side of the room.

"History," Simon added, gaze sweeping the room, "is written not just by the victors, but by the comfortable. Which is why I've decided to continue my research right here. The next installment of my series will delve even deeper. Names. Connections. Truths that reshape the narrative."

A murmur passed through the crowd. Several eyes turned toward Jack Tilley.

Beth turned to glance at him, seated near the front, looking as pleased as a man sitting atop a golden egg. He straightened in his chair, hands clasped over his knee, smiling like royalty awaiting a coronation.

"There are chapters yet to be revealed," Simon said. "And they may prove... enlightening."

Jack's chest visibly puffed.

But not everyone looked comfortable. Beth noticed Mrs. Pettigrew's eyes narrow. The mayor's assistant scribbled something into her program. A couple in the third row exchanged glances. Behind them, Alma Jensen whispered to her sister Edna, and both clutched their purses like they held secrets.

Simon sipped water. "To preserve the integrity of what I've uncovered, I'll refrain from spoilers. But know this: when history is rediscovered, it shifts the present."

Beth felt something tighten inside her. It wasn't just the mystery. It was the way he said it—as if he already knew whose foundations were cracked. She glanced at Jack again. His expression was unreadable, but too still. Too satisfied. A chill passed through her— not from the room, but from the possibility that something larger, something dangerous, was brewing beneath Windy Hollow's cobbled charm.. It was the way he said it—as if he already knew whose foundations were cracked.

"And now," Penny said brightly, stepping back up, "we'll open the floor for questions."

The crowd stirred, hands raised. One person asked about his research methods. Another about his favorite town.

"What made you choose Windy Hollow?" someone asked.

Simon smiled. "Some towns whisper their stories. Yours sings."

Charlie Lane clapped louder than anyone else. Beth noticed even the skeptical ones—Mrs. Pettigrew, Alma

Jensen—nod thoughtfully. Penny caught her eye, as if to say: He sees this place better than most of us ever have.. Yours sings."

Applause followed.

And then—

Simon stopped.

He pressed a hand to his chest.

Beth rose halfway out of her seat.

Simon blinked. Wavered.

He gasped.

And then he collapsed.

The room went silent.

A teacup shattered on the floor.

Beth was on her feet, rushing forward. Her chair clattered behind her as adrenaline surged through her limbs. The room spun slightly—voices, hands, movement—and then narrowed to Simon on the floor.

Penny dropped her notes and crouched beside him. Voices rose all around them.

"Call someone!"

"Is he breathing?"

"Move back! Give him space!"

Beth knelt on the other side. Simon's eyes fluttered open for a second—then closed. His face was pale, drawn tight with pain.

Penny grabbed his wrist, searching for a pulse. "Come on. Come on."

Manny pushed through the crowd, already on his radio. "We need EMTs at Pages & Stories. Now."

Time slowed. Beth asked "Penny, do you have a defibrillator?"

Penny shook her head, but Manny said "I have one in my car."

Manny left the shop and returned in a flash with an automatic defibrillator from his patrol vehicle, a compact case he handled with familiar urgency. The crowd parted to let him through, their chatter now replaced with tense silence and the occasional sharp breath.

"Clear the space! Everyone, back!" Manny instructed with authority, setting the case down and flipping it open. His fingers moved quickly, peeling away Simon's blazer and button-down shirt, exposing a white undershirt beneath.

Beth helped tear the fabric to reveal Simon's chest while Penny kept a steadying hand on his wrist.

"Pads—there. Monitor's live," Manny muttered, placing the sticky electrodes in their marked positions. The AED emitted a low series of beeps, and then a mechanical voice prompted, "Analyzing heart rhythm. Do not touch the patient."

Everyone in the room held their breath.

"Shock advised. Charging," the device stated.

Manny sat back slightly. "Clear!" he shouted.

He pressed the button, and Simon's body gave a slight jolt.

Beth flinched. Penny gasped but didn't move.

The AED beeped again. "Analyzing heart rhythm. Do not touch the patient."

"Still nothing," Manny said under his breath, his jaw clenched. "Come on, come on..."

"Shock not advised. Begin CPR," the device directed.

Manny didn't hesitate. He began compressions—steady, measured, precise.

Beth reached for Simon's hand. It was limp. Cold. The weight of it settled into her chest like a stone.

Manny paused for a moment and tilted Simon's head, checking for breath. Then resumed compressions.

Penny was crying now, silent tears slipping down her cheeks. "He was fine. Just minutes ago. He was fine."

Still, there was no sign of life.

When the paramedics finally arrived and took over, Beth and Penny stepped back. Manny stood, arms trembling slightly, sweat beading on his forehead.

One of the paramedics knelt, checked Simon's vitals again, and quietly conferred with the other.

Then he stood, removed his gloves, and spoke words that hit the room like a punch to the gut.

"Time of death, 11:46 a.m."

But by the time the paramedics arrived, the crowd already knew.

Simon Caldwell was gone.

Declared dead on arrival.

Penny stood at the edge of the shop, her expression blank as glass. Beth stood beside her, stunned. Around them, murmurs began again. But this time, they carried a different tone.

Not excitement.

Something closer to dread.

Windy Hollow had waited eagerly for Simon Caldwell to arrive.

Beth stood motionless. Her mind reeled—not just from grief, but from something colder. A whisper of fear that tickled the edges of her instincts.

What if this wasn't just bad luck?

Simon had hinted at buried truths, broken legacies, uncomfortable ghosts. What if someone hadn't wanted those truths unearthed?

Now they were left with more questions than answers.

Chapter 3
Sifting for Clues

The news of Simon Caldwell's death spread through Windy Hollow faster than the morning fog rolled in from the hills. By the following sunrise, the village was buzzing—but this time with whispers and wary glances instead of cheerful greetings. The usual bustle around the village square was subdued. Conversations were carried out in hushed tones over shop counters and beneath porch awnings, every whispered speculation forming a new piece of an unspoken puzzle.

Beth walked Snickers along the edge of the green, their footsteps nearly silent on the damp path. The dog trotted dutifully beside her, tail down for once. He, too, seemed to sense the shift in the village's atmosphere. Across the street, Mrs. Pettigrew stood in front of the post office, speaking lowly to Millie Carr. Both looked up as Beth passed and offered tight, sympathetic smiles.

"I can't believe it," Millie called softly. "One minute he's speaking like a prophet, the next..."

Beth gave a quiet nod. "I know."

They didn't need to finish the sentence. Everyone in town had seen it—or at least, heard about it before the hour was out.

Back at the bakery, the scent of cinnamon and coffee comforted her as she wiped down the counter for the third time that morning. But her thoughts were anywhere but settled.

"Something's not right," she whispered aloud. Snickers gave a small huff from his bed under the window.

She couldn't shake the image of Simon's face before he collapsed. That look—surprise, pain, and something else. As if he had known.

Manny's voice echoed in her memory: "We need EMTs at Pages & Stories. Now."

She pulled off her apron and tied her hair back, the way she used to when preparing for long recipe testing days. But this wasn't about baking. This was about getting answers.

At the village square, a small crowd had formed outside the mayor's office, murmuring in tight clusters. When Manny emerged, notepad in hand and brow furrowed, the voices quieted.

"Detective Piccott," Beth called gently, stepping closer.

He looked up, his expression softening when he saw her. "Beth. Hey."

"Any news?"

"Too soon. Coroner's report is pending, but I'm trying to collect statements."

"Then let me help."

Manny blinked. "Help?"

"You know everyone here," Beth said. "But I really know them. How they talk when they're relaxed, when they're lying. I can sense it. Let me ask around."

He looked at her, considering.

"Plus," she added, *"I think he was onto something. Something he didn't get to finish."*

Manny sighed. "Alright. Just... be careful. This isn't a game of Clue."

"I know. But someone might've wanted him silenced."

That afternoon, Beth returned to Pages & Stories, where Penny was already immersed in research.

"What are you doing?" Beth asked.

"I've been feeding Simon's name into COMP-AI," Penny said, not looking up from her screen. Her fingers danced across the keyboard with a focus that made Beth think she might've missed her calling as a spy—or at least a slightly sarcastic librarian version of one.

Beth raised a brow. "You and that thing. It's like watching a rom-com where the quirky best friend falls in love with a search engine."

Penny grinned. "Please. If I were going to fall for a machine, it would at least be one with a better user interface. But COMP-AI is pretty special."

She tapped the screen and spun it slightly toward Beth. "It's a deep-net AI module that pulls from surface web, archived forums, academic repositories, encrypted caches—stuff a normal search wouldn't catch in a million lifetimes of Googling. Think: Sherlock Holmes meets Bletchley Park meets a snarky high school debate team."

"So it's you in machine form."

"Flattering," Penny said. *"Though I'm not sure COMP-AI could rock a beret quite like I do."*

"Where did you learn to use this?"

"You know, a bookstore in this town is not terribly busy. I have a little spare time for cool tech," Penny said with a wink.

She turned back to her screen.

"There's a digital trail, but some of it's strange. Password-protected documents. Unusual search patterns. A few deleted posts on social media that have been cached."

Beth leaned in. "Deleted posts? From him or others?"

"From a few locals commenting on his announcement to research Windy Hollow. One even said, 'Dig too deep and you might not like what you find.'"

Beth felt a chill at the base of her neck.

"Also," Penny continued, "he was emailing a researcher from the state university history department. They were discussing something called the Founder's Vault."

"Vault?" Beth frowned. "What kind of vault?"

"No idea. But I found a note in Simon's online research log. Listen to this: 'Location uncertain. Record incomplete. Must check historical society archive—especially missing years 1907–1915.'"

Beth sat back. "You don't think it's connected to the old schoolhouse fire, do you?"

Penny's brow furrowed. "That fire was 1912. So... possibly?"

Armed with this new thread, Beth decided to weave her questions into her afternoon routine. She couldn't

*just drop everything and turn full-time investigator—
there were pastries to prep and orders to fill. But she
could take Snickers out for a walk, and in Windy
Hollow, that was often as good as an open invitation to
conversation.*

*With a leash in one hand and a small paper bag of
warm shortbread in the other, Beth meandered down
Maple Street, greeting passersby with casual smiles.
Snickers trotted happily ahead, occasionally stopping
to sniff flowerpots or wag his tail at familiar
shopkeepers. Their first stop was Greta's flower shop,
where the windows bloomed year-round thanks to both
clever arrangements and a slightly overactive radiator.*

*"Beth! These tulips just came in this morning.
You'd think spring had personally blessed them,"
Greta called as the bell jingled.*

Beth held up the shortbread. "A trade?"

Greta's eyes sparkled. "Always."

*As they nibbled and chatted, Beth steered the
conversation to Simon.*

*"He came in asking about the old homesteads on
the edge of town," Greta admitted. "Seemed genuinely
curious. I told him he should go speak with Jack TIlley.
He is the president of the Historical Society, after all,
but he looked at me and laughed. Seems like he was
somewhat contemptuous of what a town historian
could do for him".*

*Beth nodded and jotted a mental note. Greta's
remark lingered. Why had Simon been so dismissive of
Jack? Was it just academic arrogance—or something
else? Jack's reputation mattered to him. Maybe a little*

too much.. Next, she and Snickers continued toward the post office. Roger Milne, predictably, was seated at the front desk with his crossword puzzle and a cup of strong black tea.

"Hey Roger," she said casually.

"Afternoon, Miss Sanders. Here to collect or to inquire?"

Beth grinned. "Bit of both."

Roger leaned back, stretching. "I suppose this is about Caldwell? Word gets around. He had me deliver a pretty hefty envelope to him at the inn last week. Marked 'confidential,' handwritten in that loopy script of his. Seemed tired, too. Like he hadn't slept in a while. But driven. Focused. Like a man chasing ghosts."

Mrs. Pettigrew offered more cryptic commentary. "Simon was a man who stirred waters better left still."

"Why?" Beth asked gently.

"Because the truth is like yeast, dear. Once it rises, it's hard to control."

Back at the bookstore, Penny had compiled a digital profile. The familiar scent of aged pages mingled with lavender oil and a faint whiff of toasted oat biscuits—a signature of Penny's snack drawer. The hush in the air wasn't just for atmosphere anymore—it felt like holding your breath before a revelation.

"Simon was poking into Windy Hollow's founding families," she explained. "The Yates. The Pettigrews. The Stonehursts of course. Even your family, Beth."

Beth blinked. "Mine?"

"Just names in public land records, old baking contest rosters, school directories. Nothing too deep yet. But it looks like he was mapping social threads."

Beth glanced toward the bakery window from where she stood. The town looked the same. But her instincts told her the surface had barely been scratched.

"And there's more," Penny said. "I found a voice note. It's encrypted but transcribable. Listen."

A garbled recording played, then resolved: "If I can find the vault, I'll be able to verify the connections. The village kept too many secrets, but the documents—if intact—will make the whole picture clear. It's more than just names. It's who's been rewriting the story."

Beth's pulse quickened. A thrill and unease warred in her chest. "This vault… could be real."

"It could also be dangerous," Penny warned.

By evening, Beth, Penny, and Manny met again over tea and leftover pastries.

"Here's what we know," Manny said, laying out his notes. "Simon had an investigative target: village history. Possibly involving a vault. He was planning to reveal something that could change how we see Windy Hollow."

"And someone might've wanted that stopped," Beth said. "Wouldn't Mr. Tilley have some of these answers?"

"We should ask him if he knows anything about this."

Snickers barked once and pawed at a stack of research folders.

"Thank you, Assistant Detective," Beth muttered.

Just as the trio prepared to call it a night, Beth's phone buzzed. One new message.

She swiped it open.

"Digging up bones is dangerous work, even if they're made of paper."

No sender.

Her breath caught. A chill spread across her shoulders like a sudden fog.

"Someone knows we're asking questions," she said quietly.

Penny leaned in, scanning the message. "And they don't want us finding the answers."

Beth turned to Manny, who was already frowning.

He took the phone but didn't say anything. His jaw was tight.

Beth gripped her teacup, but it suddenly felt too hot to hold.

Who would even know they were this close? Her eyes flitted to the window. Nothing but shadow.

Somewhere beneath the calm of Windy Hollow, a storm was waiting...

Chapter 4
Half-Baked Histories

Beth stirred in bed the next morning, the message still echoing in her thoughts.

Digging up bones is dangerous work, even if they're made of paper.

It had arrived without a name, unsigned and cryptic, and Beth had stared at it for far too long before finally setting her phone aside the night before. She lay in bed now, sunlight pushing gently through the curtains, the soft rhythm of Snickers breathing against her leg. Outside, Windy Hollow was just beginning to stretch its limbs for the day, but Beth's thoughts were already racing.

She sat up slowly, brushing hair from her face. Something about that message didn't feel like a prank. It wasn't blunt or crude—it was calculated, as if intended to both warn and provoke. It hinted at knowledge. At intent.

As she moved to the kitchen and began brewing a small pot of coffee, her thoughts returned to Evelyn. Her mother had never shied away from uncomfortable truths. Whether it was calling out hypocrisy at the church board meetings or baking double the usual amount for families too proud to accept charity, Evelyn always believed in facing things head-on. Beth could almost hear her now: "If someone's hiding the truth, it's probably because the truth matters."

Then she thought of Graham—her husband, gone too soon. He would've told her to trust her gut, to take care of herself, and to never underestimate the power of pie in an emotional crisis. Beth smiled faintly as she poured her coffee. She missed him most in quiet moments like this, when resolve met vulnerability in a kitchen full of memories.

She wasn't backing down. If Simon's research hinted at deeper truths about Windy Hollow, she needed to unearth them.

She remembered one rainy afternoon shortly after her engagement to Graham. They'd been visiting Windy Hollow, holed up inside her mother's kitchen. Evelyn had pulled out a stack of old recipes and insisted on baking with both of them. Graham had barely known a spatula from a soup spoon, but he'd jumped in with his usual boyish enthusiasm, splattering flour on himself, on Evelyn, and finally on Beth—earning a cackle from her mother that echoed through the house like music.

"That man is a kitchen disaster," Evelyn had laughed, hands on her hips, cheeks pink from the oven heat. "He nearly buttered the bottom of the rolling pin and tried to turn it into a pie crust press."

Beth had wiped flour off her nose and grinned. "He's my havoc."

"Well, good. I raised you to appreciate quality mayhem," Evelyn had replied. "Now make sure he doesn't mistake the powdered sugar for flour again, or we'll end up with a cake that tastes like an old slipper covered in fondant."

"Is it too late to elope and spare him this trauma?"

"You're assuming I'd let you leave without dessert. Priorities, dear."

It was one of those golden memories, suspended in time—the kind that wrapped around you like a soft blanket on a cold morning. Graham had believed in her when she didn't believe in herself. And Evelyn had made sure Beth knew that building something—whether a relationship or a bakery—was always worth the mess.

That memory filled her now. Courage didn't always look like grand gestures. Sometimes, it meant asking questions—even when the answers scared you.

Later that morning, Beth slipped on her walking shoes and clipped the leash onto Snickers' collar. "Let's do some snooping, subtle-like," she said, giving the corgi a scratch behind the ears. He wagged his tail and trotted happily beside her as they stepped into the early spring air.

As they strolled through the village, the warmth of the sun brightened stone façades and flower boxes. It was market day, and stalls were already being set up along the green. Beth nodded to Peter Albright, who was arranging jars of honey beside a table of woven baskets.

"Mornin', Beth," Peter called. "Your lemon bars were the talk of the town yesterday. Mrs. Tims swears they cured her allergies."

"That or the eucalyptus," Beth laughed. "Good turnout today."

"Everyone's still buzzing about that book event. Shame about Caldwell."

"It is," Beth said, and after a pause, added, "You ever hear of something called the Founder's Vault?"

Peter blinked. "That an insurance company?"

Beth grinned. "Never mind."

She moved on. Every stop was a small opportunity—chatting with Marlene, the hairdresser, who claimed her grandfather once found a hidden tunnel beneath the old meeting hall; listening to a pair of teenagers speculate that Caldwell's death was part of a secret society conspiracy.

Outside the bakery, Beth paused as she passed Mr. Albright, the retired postmaster, talking to Miss Lydia.

"You hear what happened at Pages & Stories?" he murmured, not quietly enough.

"Of course I did," Lydia replied. "And if Beth Sanders had an ounce of self-preservation, she'd leave history where it belongs."

Beth slowed her pace. She wasn't supposed to hear it. And yet, now she couldn't unhear it.

She jotted down notes on her phone whenever she could. Most of it was silly, exaggerated, or misremembered. But she knew from baking: even a perfect recipe can start with odd ingredients.

Midday brought her back to the bakery. She'd barely tied her apron when a familiar knock sounded at the door. Jack Tilley.

"Beth! Afternoon," he said with his usual polished charm. "Here to pick up scones for the Historical

Society luncheon. Nothing gets people excited about heritage like lemon glaze."

Beth handed him the paper bag. "Fresh batch. You'll be the most popular person there."

"That or the coffee cake," Jack said. "We're holding the luncheon at the parish hall. Not exactly historical, but it'll do. It went up after the big fire wiped out the original courthouse, so the bones are newer than most places around here."

She smiled politely. "Well, lemon glaze should help jog their memories."

He chuckled. "As long as they remember the society exists, I'm happy."

She leaned on the counter casually. "Mr. Tilley, have you ever heard about a Chamber Nine? Some kind of sealed archive?"

Jack's brow furrowed briefly, then relaxed. "Ah, one of our many ghost stories. Hilda's probably told you all about it. Some forgotten cellar supposedly hidden beneath the old courthouse. We did find something years ago—tiny room filled with old sketches and broken shelves. Looked more like a janitor's closet than a vault."

Beth kept her expression easy. "So no hidden documents with scandalous revelations?"

He laughed. "If there were, I would've already published a commemorative pamphlet. Trust me, Beth. Windy Hollow's past is charming, but not particularly thrilling."

She smiled politely, watching him go. Jack exuded confidence on all things historical—and in Windy

Hollow, that was currency. He was the president of the Historical Society and practically Windy Hollow's unofficial archivist. His knowledge came from decades of family stories, documented minutes, and the occasional ribbon-cutting ceremony speech. He probably had every newsletter from the last fifty years tucked in his attic.

Still, Beth couldn't help but wonder—was it possible even Jack didn't know everything? Not out of secrecy, but maybe because his methods, though earnest, were limited. Penny had once said that relying solely on local lore was old school, like trying to map a galaxy with binoculars on a cloudy night. COMP-AI, on the other hand, was like launching a telescope into orbit.

Beth tucked the thought away as she walked back to the storeroom. The Founder's Vault could very well be a dusty legend passed around like a ghost story at the Green. But Simon had believed it was something more. And Beth was beginning to think he might have been right.

Later that afternoon, Beth joined Penny at Pages & Stories. The bell above the door jingled as she entered, and Penny glanced up from behind a mountain of books and a half-empty mug of coffee.

"Tell me you brought snacks," Penny said.

"Mini muffins and the tiniest lead you've ever heard of," Beth replied.

They settled at the back reading nook, Snickers sprawled out across their feet. Penny had already set aside several local history books and a stack of old newsletters, her laptop humming quietly beside her with COMP-AI still running in the background.

"What? You're reading ink on paper?" Beth asked with mock surprise, leaning on the armrest like she was about to stage a literary intervention.

"Don't act like I've betrayed the algorithm," Penny shot back. "Even the best AI needs context. COMP-AI only knows what it's been fed. Sometimes, the secrets are buried in boxes no one's bothered to digitize."

"So basically, you're Indiana Jones, but with metadata."

"Exactly," Penny said. "And this—" she flipped open a crisp folder and slid it across the table "—is the Holy Grail of 1976."

Beth raised a brow. "A centennial program?"

"With a hidden gem on the back page. Behold, a speech by then-Mayor Roland Greene."

She tapped the section triumphantly. "He mentions a time capsule—stored in something called Chamber Nine. Could be the same as the Founder's Vault."

Beth gave a low whistle. "Mr. Tilley really might've missed this." The quote about safeguarding records wasn't just nostalgic—it hinted at something deeper. Were those traditions meant to protect the records... or hide them?

"I've got COMP-AI cross-referencing scanned documents with OCR-flagged town records, local newspapers, and a disturbingly thorough genealogy blog written by someone named 'HistoricalHarriet87.'"

"Wow," Beth said, impressed. "And here I thought I was productive when I refilled the salt jars."

"To be fair, I needed a break after nearly burning out my CPU chasing a red herring about a Pettigrew second cousin who turned out to be a magician from Ohio."

Beth grinned. "You've got the AI. I've got muffins. Together, we're unstoppable.".

"Jack's a human encyclopedia," Penny said, sipping her lukewarm coffee. "But encyclopedias go out of date. COMP-AI doesn't. He can quote town ordinances from the 1800s, but if something wasn't typed and filed at town hall or shouted across the church lawn in the '80s, he doesn't consider it reliable."

"So we're the 'unreliable narrators' Mr. Tilley never fact-checked?"

"Basically."

Beth exhaled slowly. "Okay. What do we know about this Roland Greene?"

"He served one term, very civic-minded. Retired to Florida and raised parakeets. But that's not the point. The point is, he referenced it publicly. So it's not just a myth."

Beth sat back. "If Simon was chasing the same reference... it's possible he uncovered more."

Penny nodded. "And he was tying it to founding families—likely to expose patterns. I've been rereading some of Simon's annotations. Look."

She opened a scanned file and zoomed in on a handwritten margin note: 'Chamber Nine = origin key?'

"He was tracking this for a while," Beth whispered. Her pulse ticked upward. Was someone else already looking for this? Could the danger Simon faced still linger for them?

That evening, the trio gathered again at the bakery after hours. Manny leaned against the prep table while Beth handed him a slice of rhubarb tart. "You realize we sound like the town's least intimidating secret society, right?"

"Please," Penny said, adjusting her glasses. "We're at least the second least intimidating. The garden club once declared herbicide on a rival over who planted lavender on the library lawn."

"They nearly made national news," Beth added, pouring tea. "Tulip Turf War of Windy Hollow."

"Okay, fair. We're third least intimidating," Manny conceded.

"So, the Founder's Vault might be real," Manny said.

"Chamber Nine," Penny corrected. "Or both. Or aliases for something else."

"Simon believed there was something important hidden—documents, relics. Something tied to Windy Hollow's past."

Manny scribbled in his notebook. "Then I'll check building records tomorrow. Maybe something's been mislabeled or sealed off."

"Meanwhile," Beth said, "we keep digging. Discreetly."

As they wrapped up, Penny flipped through a weathered village publication.

"Wait," she murmured. "Here. Look at this."

She pointed to a faded paragraph in an anniversary booklet from the 1950s.

'Following the fire of 1912, which gutted the schoolhouse and badly damaged neighbouring buildings—including the town archives, the courthouse and the old mayor's residence—records and valuables were moved and stored elsewhere in town. Though several townspeople suffered burns and smoke inhalation, no lives were lost thanks to the swift response of the Windy Hollow volunteer fire brigade. Many said it was a miracle. The location of these salvaged records became known to few but was protected by tradition and trusted hands.'

Beth leaned forward. "That's not just poetic," she murmured. "It's a breadcrumb. A hint that we're heading in the right direction."

They looked at each other, understanding passing silently.

There was more beneath Windy Hollow than any of them had imagined.

Chapter 5

The Secret Ingredient

Beth never imagined starting her morning in a bookstore nook, eating a blueberry muffin while dissecting search engine algorithms over laptop glow. Yet here she was at Pages & Stories, tucked into the shop's coziest nook—complete with a faded patchwork armchair and the faint scent of old paper—wedged between Jay and Lex, Windy Hollow's youngest tech enthusiasts and self-appointed digital sherpas. Snickers, ever the opportunist, had attempted to climb into Jay's lap twice, convinced the glowing laptop screen was obviously hiding a biscuit.

"Okay, this bakery needs a personality," Jay said, adjusting his round glasses and typing furiously.

"I thought that was me," Beth said, sipping her tea.

"It is," Lex chimed in. "But your muffins don't have a Twitter account, and we can fix that. People want content that's warm, inviting, and slightly crazy. Just like your kitchen."

Beth glanced down at Snickers sprawled under the table with flour still clinging to his ear. "So, like the muffin version of a corgi with boundary issues?"

"Exactly," Jay grinned.

They showed her how to build stories around her baked goods—photos of cooling pies with quirky captions, short videos of frosting fails, polls on whether cinnamon or cardamom should be the dominant spice in coffee cake. All of it was fun, playful, and rooted in her voice.

By mid-morning, the bakery had an Instagram, a Facebook feed filled with behind-the-scenes clips, and a TikTok video of Snickers hauling a loaf almost as big as he was—already climbing toward three hundred views.

Beth smiled at the growing engagement, but part of her mind stayed fixed on another kind of digital presence.

In the reading nook, Penny had her laptop open, COMP-AI humming away with new queries.

Beth settled in with a fresh cup of lemon balm tea. "What are you running now?"

Penny didn't look up. "Just combing back through some of Simon's online activity logs. Email headers, forum activity, saved article drafts—anything we might've missed before. Nothing classified, just publicly accessible stuff with a little creative searching."

"You make it sound like you're hacking into the Pentagon."

Penny smirked. "Please. This is child's play. I once found an entire deleted manuscript buried inside a book club newsletter's RSS feed."

Beth shook her head. "That's either deeply impressive or mildly terrifying."

Penny grinned. "Why not both?"

Snickers snored in his sleep, stretching out and nudging Beth's ankle. Then, as if on cue, one of his back legs kicked out mid-dream and caught the laptop cord, nearly yanking it from Penny's lap.

"Hey! Down, Agent Snickers," Penny muttered, righting the screen.

Beth laughed. "I think he's dreaming about chasing conspiracy theories."

"Or squirrels who know too much," Penny said, patting his head.

COMP-AI gave a gentle chime.

Penny leaned in. 'Here we go—Simon's digital ghost left a trail the night before his speech—encrypted messages, but they were routed through public IPs. Not his usual pattern. He also accessed the county's digital land records, but the searches were oddly generic—broad terms, weird phrasing. Penny tapped the screen, highlighting one particular filename.

"This one's labeled 'LandLot_ChamberRef_alt.txt'—it was downloaded to his local drive, but never emailed or uploaded. If I hadn't checked the cached auto-saves, we'd never know it existed."

Beth frowned. "What's in it?"

"It's messy," Penny admitted. "Mostly notes—references to Chamber Nine, and a cross-comparison of surnames tied to land deeds from 1908 through 1914. Looks like he was connecting a web of names—possibly trying to flag discrepancies in how ownership shifted after the fire."

Beth blinked. "So he might've found something. Something big.""

Beth leaned in. "Can you tell who he was messaging?"

"Unfortunately no—the recipient's info is anonymized. But I can see keywords in the subject lines."

"Let me guess," Beth said. "a vault?"

"That, and two others: inheritance and misattribution."

Beth blinked. "You know, that reminds me of the old rumor about the Dunsmore family deed being forged. Didn't Mrs. Pettigrew once claim it was signed in crayon?"

Penny snorted. "Yes, and she also insists her rosebush is descended from Marie Antoinette's garden. But hey, who am I to question botanical royalty?"

"Still," Beth said, stirring her tea, "sometimes those old whispers carry a kernel of truth—or at least enough to send someone scrambling to hide their paperwork.""

Penny nodded. "Exactly. And based on how sloppy the digital trail is for someone normally precise like Simon, I'd say he was either rushed… or scared."

"Actually," Penny said, squinting at the screen, "COMP-AI did flag one weird outlier—some scanned correspondence with a Winifred Beckley in Ohio. It's all about a traveling magic show and a missing ledger from a town two counties over."

Beth raised an eyebrow. "You think Simon was onto something?"

Penny shook her head. "Nope. Turns out it was a false link—she was researching circus fraud for her novel. But for a hot second, I thought Simon was following a magician."

They gathered that afternoon in the bakery's kitchen. Manny was off-duty but still wore his badge, as if this mystery needed his whole self present.

"I'm telling you," Beth said, laying out a stack of Simon's notes, "he wasn't just tracing lineage—he was looking at implications. Who claimed what, and maybe shouldn't have."

Manny flipped through a page. "Dense stuff. He keeps circling a land grant filed in 1908—right around the time of the fire."

"Which," Penny added, "might've been why those records were stored in the Founder's Vault."

"And now they're either missing or hidden," Beth said.

"Any word from the coroner?" she asked.

Manny nodded, his face tightening. "Preliminary report says no trauma or clear cause. Toxicology's pending—but in context, it raises flags."

"Toxicology?" Penny's brow furrowed. "So we're thinking poison?"

"Possibly," Manny said. "We won't know anything definitive until results come back. But if there was something in his system, it could take a few days to show up."

He paused, the line of his jaw tightening. "He stopped by the station the day before. Dropped off a copy of his manuscript. Said I should read it sometime."

Beth sat back. "He didn't seem sick. Just intense."

There was a beat of silence.

Manny glanced up. "Are we saying someone's rewriting Windy Hollow's history?"

Beth raised an eyebrow. "A bakery can survive scandal. But can a town?"

Penny raised her teacup. "To revisionist muffins."

The next day, after morning prep, Beth slipped on her coat and leash in hand, decided to walk Snickers down the quieter side streets. She needed air, and thinking space.

Snickers darted from flowerpot to lamppost, wagging his tail at anything that moved. Beth tugged him gently toward the edge of the Green, where the path curled around the back of the inn.

She paused, looking up at the workshed, half-charred but still standing. Its roof sagged a little more than yesterday.

A gust of wind blew past. She took another step—and that's when she heard it.

A sudden crack.

Beth looked up.

A brick tumbled from the upper story balcony.

It struck the ground inches from her foot with a sharp thud, chipping the pavement.

Snickers barked, startled. Beth stumbled back, heart thudding.

She looked up again. No one was on the balcony. The windows were dark.

Accident?

Beth crouched and studied the brick. Too precise. Too close. Her hands trembled as she called Snickers back to her side and tightened the leash.

She wasn't hurt—but someone had wanted her to notice. A window curtain on the second floor swayed slightly, though no wind stirred from below. There was no sound, no further movement—only the rustling of early spring leaves and her own heartbeat pounding in her ears. It could've been a fluke. Or it could've been something else. Something—or someone—watching?

Back at the bakery, she recounted the incident to Manny and Penny over a quiet pot of chamomile tea.

"Could've been a fluke," Manny said. "But I'll take a look."

"I don't like it," Penny said. "A possible poisoning, and now this? We are past subtle warnings."

Beth nodded. "Which means we're getting closer."

They sat in the bakery's back office that evening, surrounded by notes, baked goods, and warm lighting. Snickers lay curled up beneath the desk, breathing slow and steady.

"Here's the plan," Manny said. "I'll follow the building permit trail. Penny, dig further into Simon's land grant references. Beth, keep listening—casually. Sometimes the locals say more than they realize. But both of you—be careful, please."

Beth nodded. "I'm good at casual listening. It's my specialty. Right behind casual eavesdropping and passive-aggressive pie baking."

"I've seen your judgmental crusts," Penny said. "They haunt me."

Beth smirked. "That lemon chess pie I made for the Harvest Fair two years ago? Totally aimed at Edna Myers. She said my streusel was 'emotionally flat.' So I made sure that pie crust had more attitude than her entire book club."

They laughed, and Manny stood, gathering his things.

"I'll check in with you both tomorrow," he said. "Seriously—watch your backs."

He gave Snickers a gentle scratch behind the ears and let himself out through the front door.

Beth and Penny remained, quietly sorting papers and tidying the space. As Beth reached for her coat hanging by the bakery's front door, her foot brushed against something.

"What's that?" Penny asked.

Beth bent down and spotted an envelope, half-tucked under the welcome mat. The corner was damp, curling slightly. No stamp. Just her name—clean, sharp, deliberate.

She opened it cautiously.

Inside was a single sheet of paper, typed:

Leave well enough alone. You don't want to be next.

Beth read the words aloud.

The room fell silent.

Penny crossed the room in three quick strides and gently took the letter, flipping it over. Nothing.

"We need to give this to Manny," she said, already reaching for her phone.

Beth held up a hand. "Wait. If we do that, he'll shut us down. He'll tell us to stay out of it, maybe even stop looking altogether. And if someone went to the trouble of delivering this to me... we're closer than we thought."

Penny looked at her for a long moment, then slowly set the phone down.

Snickers chewed at an old ball, oblivious to the tension in the room.

Beth folded the note carefully, her fingers trembling slightly.

Whoever left it knew exactly where to find her. And they wanted her afraid.

She wasn't ready to be afraid just yet.

Whatever they were nearing, someone clearly wanted it buried.

And now she was sure—they were closer than she thought.

Chapter 6

Whisked Together

The rain began softly, like a whisper. It tapped gently against the windowpanes of the bakery, tracing delicate streams along the glass and pooling on the cobbled streets outside. Inside, the scent of coffee, cinnamon, and rising bread wrapped around Beth like a blanket. A few regulars trickled in, the bell above the door chiming softly each time. The bakery felt like a sanctuary from the world's complications—cozy, warm, safe. But Beth knew better than to confuse atmosphere with reality.

Standing at the front window, she wrapped her hands around her favorite chipped mug, the scent of warm cinnamon rolls curling through the air like a hug. Outside, a bicycle bell rang, followed by the soft splashing of cart wheels over rain-slicked cobblestones and the distant clang of church chimes marking the hour. The comfort of the bakery's familiar rhythms clashed with the storm brewing inside her. Unanswered questions stirred unease, and the creeping sense that Windy Hollow' peace was only skin-deep lingered. Steam curled toward her face. She took a slow sip of lemon ginger tea and stared out at the fog-draped square, her reflection ghosted on the glass beside Snickers' curious, upturned face.

"Still nothing new from the coroner," she murmured. Snickers sneezed faintly in response.

She closed her eyes briefly, breathing in the calm before another storm.

"I miss you, Graham," she whispered. "I could use your take on all of this... or at least a really good breakfast sandwich."

By late morning, Penny met her at Pages & Stories. The rain had tapered off to a gentle drizzle, and the bookstore smelled of old pages and damp coats. Penny wore a teal rain jacket and fingerless gloves, and Snickers, damp and mildly annoyed, shook off water by the umbrella stand with a flourish.

"Alright, librarian detective mode activated," Penny announced, tossing her gloves on the counter. "Let's dig."

They pulled old newspapers from the archive stacks in the back, though Snickers, clearly not briefed on proper archival protocol, plopped down squarely on a 1974 issue. Beth gently nudged him aside, biting back a laugh. Together, they leafed through old papers, occasionally exclaiming when they found a forgotten council scandal or a cringe-worthy letter to the editor about sidewalk etiquette.

Beth tapped the edge of a 1982 special edition. "Here. Look at this article. It's about the Stonehurst land dispute. It mentions rumors of a sealed vault—no name, but it sounds familiar."

Penny leaned in. "That's the year they moved the library. Could the vault have been under the original site?"

"Maybe Simon found something tying it back."

They continued reading until Penny let out a triumphant, "Aha!" She held up a small, water-damaged notebook wedged between issues. The cover was cracked, but inside was Simon's handwriting. The ink was faded but urgent, a record of thoughts preserved—and hidden, just like so much else in Windy Hollow.

"It's not much," she said, flipping pages. "But this—" she pointed to a coded sequence of symbols scribbled in the margins, "—isn't gibberish. Simon left a key somewhere."

Beth peered at the symbols: a mix of shapes, letters, and what looked like recipe shorthand. "Please tell me he didn't write it in pie crust code."

"If he did, we're consulting your lemon chess pie," Penny said. "It's vengeful and revealing."

Over lunch back at the bakery, the two women sat with bowls of lentil soup, crusty bread, and mugs of coffee. Just as Beth was about to ladle a second helping for Penny, the bell above the bakery door jingled.

"Afternoon, Beth! Smells like trust and calories in here," called Ernest Mulrooney, Windy Hollow's semi-retired chimney sweep and full-time storyteller. His tweed cap dripped with rainwater, and his raincoat looked older than the town charter.

"Come in before you melt," Beth called, already grabbing a clean napkin.

Ernest sniffed the air. "Is that lentil? You've saved me from canned soup despair."

"You're in luck. We have space and spoons."

As he settled onto a nearby stool, Ernest tapped the table and grinned. "You know, I once stumbled on a room beneath the old mill—thought it was a vault for about five seconds."

Penny raised a brow. "A vault?"

"Well, more of a root cellar, really. Padlock and dust though, which in my book makes it mysterious."

Beth laughed. "Did it contain ancient secrets?"

"Three broken brooms, a stack of catalogs from 1969, and a raccoon who did not want visitors. But you never know with these old buildings."

As Ernest slurped his soup, the trio exchanged amused glances. A classic Windy Hollow moment—full of lore, misdirection, and a dash of raccoon-infused drama.

They returned to their notes, theories punctuated now with laughter and the occasional spoon clink. For a brief moment, amidst the layers of mystery, they were grounded again in community., crusty bread, and mugs of coffee. Manny joined them with a box of case notes and an appetite that suggested he hadn't eaten all day.

"Did you ever solve the Mystery of the Jammed Council Door?" Penny teased.

Manny shrugged. "Turns out it was locked. With a key. By the person inside. Mystery solved."

Beth chuckled. "Windy Hollow's very own noir series."

"Small towns are breeding grounds for tiny mysteries," Manny said between spoonfuls. "Lost cats, stolen garden gnomes, competitive composting. This just happens to be one with higher stakes."

They turned back to the notes, sharing theories and laughter in equal measure. For a moment, despite the darkness pressing at the edges of their investigation, things felt normal.

The bell above the bakery door chimed.

Manny stood. "Be right back. I owe Carol at Dusty Relics a favor—she said she found something on those building records."

Beth raised a brow. "Carol? The same Carol who tried to charge me seventy-five dollars for a rusted egg beater because it 'had provenance'?"

"Exactly," Manny said with a grin. "Wish me luck."

He returned fifteen minutes later with a furrowed brow and a barely concealed grimace.

"Let me guess," Penny said. "She tried to sell you your own birth certificate."

"Close. She waved a handwritten receipt dated 1913 in my face, claiming it proves the Tilley family sold property under mysterious circumstances. I asked for corroboration, and she threatened to hex my garage door."

"So Carol's back on the suspect list," Beth said, smirking.

"Or she's just eccentric," Manny sighed. "But it's something."

That afternoon, as rain began to fall again, Beth walked to the market. The usual smiles were more *reserved. Conversations quieted when she passed. A few villagers nodded politely and moved along.*

At first, she thought she imagined it. But after the third hesitant glance and a fourth awkward silence, she knew something was shifting.

"I heard she's been digging around old family records," someone whispered near the preserves stand.

"Simon Caldwell was nice," another murmured. "Shame what happened."

Beth clutched her shopping bag tighter. She remembered when she'd first returned to Windy Hollow and Greta had left a bouquet of wild irises at her doorstep with a note that read, 'Welcome home—this place missed you.'

She had come a long way from that first tentative morning behind the bakery counter.

These people had cheered on her bakery dreams and trusted her with their birthdays, anniversaries, and bad days only a good scone could mend. They'd trusted her with their birthdays, anniversaries, and hangovers—but maybe not with their secrets. Maybe those were reserved for people who didn't ask so many questions.

Back at the bakery, she stood by the prep table, watching the storm begin through the rear windows.

She felt the doubt creep in. Was she really helping? Or stirring up trouble that didn't want to be stirred?

Still unsettled from the glances at the market, she slipped inside the bakery, shaking rain from her coat. Her sanctuary didn't feel quite so safe anymore. Was she really helping? Or stirring up trouble that didn't want to be stirred?

She rested her hand on the countertop. "Mom… what would you do?"

She could almost hear Evelyn's response: "Bake first. Then ask the hard questions. One helps you think, the other makes people talk."

That evening, the three gathered again for tea and toast.

Penny laid out the coded diary and Simon's old notes. "You know who might actually remember something about this?" she added. "Miss Lydia—the piano teacher with the terrifying cat and the encyclopedic memory. I swear, she once recited the town's entire council roster from 1962."

Beth raised an eyebrow. "Is that the same Miss Lydia who won't play anything composed after 1890 because she considers it 'too jazzy'?"

"That's the one," Penny said. "She's eccentric, but sharp. And she was good friends with the late Mayor Greene. If anyone remembers the origins of Chamber Nine, she might."

Manny groaned. "Last time I interviewed her, she offered me stale biscotti and then lectured me for twenty minutes about the lack of classical music appreciation in law enforcement."

Beth laughed. "Sounds like we're sending Penny.". Manny flipped open a town planning book. Beth poured steaming water into a teapot shaped like a barn.

"So here's the new plan," Penny said. "We treat Simon's coded notes like a recipe. A series of steps. If we can find the key—maybe in his files, or even an old map—we follow the trail."

"We need to talk to more people," Manny added. "Especially older residents. Someone might remember something useful."

Beth nodded. "I can loop it into bakery conversation. Pie makes people open up."

Snickers barked once, looking toward the window. His ears perked and a low growl rumbled in his throat, unusual for the typically mellow corgi. Beth turned just in time to see a flash of movement outside—or maybe it was just the shadows dancing from the lightning. Still, the hairs on her arms stood on end.

Lightning flashed, illuminating the room.

"Great," Beth muttered. "A dramatic thunderstorm. As if we needed more foreshadowing."

Thunder rolled. Rain lashed the windows.

Snickers whined again.

Outside, shadows danced across the square.

Inside, the three leaned over a page marked with strange symbols and an address that had long since disappeared from any modern map.

Beth tightened her grip on the page. Whatever Simon had uncovered, they were on the same path now—and someone wasn't ready for them to reach the end.

But the storm—literal and figurative—was just beginning.

Chapter 7

Folding in the Truth

The mist rolled in like a secret whispered across Windy Hollow.

Beth stood in the kitchen doorway, a muffin tin in one hand and her notebook in the other, watching morning fog curl around lampposts and storefronts. The scent of fresh blueberry muffins floated through the air, mixing with the earthy smell of damp stone and early blossoms.

She set the muffins down and opened the notebook. Etched into the corner in Evelyn's old, looping script were the initials E.S. It was the last gift her mother had given her before she passed—a blank book, meant for recipes, maybe even business plans. But Beth had filled it with thoughts, notes, and fragments of the mystery that had engulfed their small village.

"Okay, Mom," she whispered, touching the edge of the page. "We're getting close now. Hope you're somewhere with good tea and a front-row seat."

Snickers let out a yawn from his bed under the front counter, one ear flopping over his eyes.

Later that morning, Penny arrived with a tote bag full of supplies and an iced coffee balanced precariously on top.

"I brought caffeine, a fresh mind, and two pens that may or may not be trying to ruin my pockets," she said, dropping her bag with a theatrical sigh.

Beth chuckled. "Let's hope they can help us solve family secrets and not summon ghosts."

"I make no promises."

They returned to the archive chamber—what they had started referring to as "the tomb" with equal parts reverence and sarcasm. Inside, they began flipping through boxes of dusty records and brittle sheets of parchment.

After about an hour, Beth stilled.

"Penny. Look at this."

She held up a genealogy chart, delicate and yellowed with age. Names spiraled outward— founding family trees like the Dunstons, the Greenes, and the Pettigrews were all meticulously documented. The Tilleys were nowhere to be found.

"That tracks," Beth murmured. "The Tilleys didn't arrive until about 60 years ago."

"Really? So why do people treat them like original founders?" Beth asked, squinting at the page.

"Because they've been woven in," Penny said. "For generations. They sponsor historical exhibits, chair the festival committee, and donate to every plaque and painting that's gone up downtown. They've grafted themselves onto Windy Hollow's roots. Most people wouldn't think to question it."

Beth nodded slowly. "Which is why Simon did. He was digging beneath the story everyone accepted."

"They've always been prominent," Penny said, narrowing her eyes. "Which means they should be recorded. This kind of omission isn't accidental." She flipped through another folder. "Wait—something promising… oh. Never mind. Just a merchant invoice with a familiar name."

Beth smirked. "We almost uncovered the great tomato tax conspiracy of 1903." She flipped another page. Her eyes landed on a strange symbol—what looked like a teacup.

"Okay," she said slowly, "either someone was doodling out of boredom, or this symbol means something."

Penny leaned in. "That's the third time I've seen that. Once in Simon's notebook, once on the corner of a map, and now here."

"A secret society of tea drinkers?" Beth offered.

"If only. I could finally wear that velvet cape."

They returned to the bakery by noon, arms full of documents. Manny was already there, stationed at the counter with a cinnamon bun and a look of wary amusement. The bakery smelled of cardamom and warmth, but Beth's mind was still chasing threads from the archive. They'd found pieces—but the whole picture remained elusive.

"I see research snacks are still part of your strategy," he said.

"Fuel for the truth," Penny replied.

They sat around a booth, the table cluttered with printouts, highlighters, and mugs.

Beth spread out one of the genealogy charts. "The Greenes and Pettigrews are practically mapped down to their great-uncles' shoe sizes, but something about the Yates tree feels… off."

Penny nodded. "There's a blank next to a sibling in Elliott's line—no birthdate, no spouse, just a gap. Like someone was edited out."

Manny squinted at the page. "That could mean anything. Disputed parentage? Scandal? Family feud over the last slice of funeral pie?"

"Still," Beth said, tapping the margin, "if Simon was chasing a missing link or trying to verify a claim, maybe he started here."

Penny leaned forward. "Maybe he started with the Greenes or Yates and stumbled onto something much bigger."

"As in, a carefully buried branch of the family tree?" Manny said.

Beth nodded. "And someone might've trimmed it for a reason."

As the conversation turned serious, so did the bond between them. Stories were swapped—Penny's disastrous attempt at making marshmallows, Manny's short-lived career as a middle school ventriloquist. Laughter warmed the bakery's corners, and the tension eased.

But even after the bakery had quieted, Beth's thoughts wouldn't. The puzzle was too close, the pieces too tempting. She needed to see if something important had been hiding in plain sight all along.

Later that afternoon, Beth sat down at her laptop, a cooling cup of tea beside her and Simon's disorganized notes spread across the table. Rain pattered lightly against the windowpane behind her, but she hardly noticed.

Frustration simmered beneath her calm. The coroner's report had finally confirmed what they'd all feared: poisoning. Not a heart attack, not a tragic coincidence. Murder. They still didn't know what kind—testing was still underway—but it was progress. Except they were no closer to figuring out who had done it.

Beth flipped through Simon's notes again. It was like reading a recipe without ingredients—fragmented, cryptic, and infuriating. He had threads, connections, tantalizing hints about legacies and buried truths... but no clear map. They were getting closer, but it still wasn't enough. Beth needed something Simon had seen—but hadn't spelled out.

"Well, at least I know it wasn't my muffins," she muttered, glancing at Snickers, who blinked at her from under the table.

If Simon had been poisoned, it had to have happened recently. Most likely at the signing. That narrowed things to people in the room—founders, their descendants, locals with histories that went back further than the wallpaper in town hall.

Beth pulled out the binder where she'd begun organizing possible motives.

The Stonehursts—tied to the old land scandal. The Greenes—two family members had been left out of the public records for unexplained reasons. The Yates— discrepancies in their genealogy, missing names, whispered rivalries. Even the Pettigrews, long considered respectable, had that odd generational gap with no records between 1910 and 1920.

The Founders' Vault—or Chamber Nine, or whatever it was—had turned up little more than moldy maps and metaphors. Simon had clearly believed it was key, but all they had now were symbols, partial clues, and a teacup motif that might as well have been a doodle.

And the discrepancies in the town's genealogical tree? They existed—but they didn't match anything conclusive from Simon's notes.

Beth leaned back, groaning. "This entire town is built on unsolved riddles."

Feeling restless, she clicked open the genealogy site Simon had bookmarked.

Half an hour later, she was still clicking. Half-baked family trees, migration patterns, census records—all familiar names. She started with her own out of curiosity, typing in 'Sanders.' The results surprised her. There were bakers in nearly every generation, a lineage of dough and spice stretching back to colonial days. Her great-great-grandmother, it turned out, had once won a regional baking medal with a peach cobbler so legendary it made a newspaper in Asheville. Beth smiled—it felt right. She wasn't just carrying on a tradition. She was living in it.

Like a good recipe, truth didn't always reveal itself all at once. The best flavors were the ones simmered slowly—uncovered layer by layer, with patience.

Then she turned her focus to the founding families.

The Greenes? Beth traced their branches with a practiced eye. There was a suspiciously vague marriage record in 1894—a groom listed only by initials, and a bride who appeared in no other local documents. Curious, she thought. That might suggest a marriage the family didn't want highlighted. And in the margins of an old census, one Greene child had a birth year curiously scratched out and rewritten. Mistake—or deliberate correction?

The Pettigrews? A long chain of teachers, ministers, and apothecaries. Neat, unimpeachable—and almost too clean. Beth had always found Mrs. Pettigrew's insistence on her family's moral high ground a little too polished. She flagged a curious footnote attached to a property dispute in 1911 where a Pettigrew ancestor had apparently accused a Greene of fraud—an incident quietly settled and never mentioned again in any formal record.

Before moving on, Beth took a detour out of pure mischief and typed in 'Whittaker.' Penny might not forgive her, but she couldn't help herself. To her amusement, Penny's great-great-aunt had been married twice—once to a traveling opera singer, and later to a circus knife thrower. Beth made a mental note to bring that up at their next tea.

She searched 'Piccott' next and chuckled when a note popped up linking Manny's family to a well-documented moonshine incident during Prohibition. That explained his mysterious distaste for peach schnapps.

She sighed. None of these seemed scandalous enough to go to extreme measures to silence Simon. What were they missing?

She leaned back in her chair, rubbing her temples. Maybe there wasn't a connection. Maybe all these stories were just that—unrelated threads in an old patchwork quilt, and Simon had been chasing shadows. What if they'd gotten it wrong?

But even as the doubt flickered, something deeper pushed her forward.

Beth hovered over the keyboard, fingers still for a long moment. The Stonehursts were ancient history— gone from Windy Hollow for decades, their name spoken only in whispers or half-joking warnings during historical tours. There was no real reason to look them up now. But curiosity, that age-old trait that got bakers to try savory scones and sleuths to press one step further, finally won out. If Simon had been sniffing around the Stonehurst legacy, maybe there was something worth finding.

After all, even the most withered branches of a family tree can bear rotten fruit.

She typed in the name and began tracing the family lines. There were Stonehursts as far back as the Mayflower, it seems. Further, even. She found the collection of Stonehursts in the Windy Hollow area, and that line petered out just after the 1960s. Thaddeus and Meredith Stonehurst were the last in that particular line and they had one child, no name listed and no further information present. Just a blank silhouette and a big question mark graphic. They would have been part of the generation of Stonehursts expelled from town in the early 1900s; they settled elsewhere with their ill gotten gains.

Beth frowned.

She opened two more tabs, cross-referencing names and birthplaces—until she spotted a message thread under the Stonehurst label.

She blinked.

"No way..."

She looked up the user messaging Patty Stonehurst and their family name, double-checked, then cross-checked again.

Beth pressed a hand to her chest just as thunder rolled overhead, rattling the bakery windows. Beth didn't flinch. Snickers ran for cover under her legs. She just stared at the screen, heart pounding.

"Oh my God," she whispered. "I know who did it."

Chapter 8

Burnt at the Edges

Beth barely slept.

She'd found the message thread the night before—names, DNA matches, whispers of history rewritten. She'd almost run straight to Penny's house with her laptop. But it had been too late—and too risky.

Now, the fog drifted through Windy Hollow like a whispered warning. It curled around porch posts and lampposts, heavy with unspoken tension.

Beth stirred in bed, the message still echoing in her thoughts. She sat up slowly, brushing hair from her face. Something about that message didn't feel like a prank. It wasn't blunt or crude—it was calculated, as if intended to both warn and provoke. It hinted at knowledge. At intent.

She couldn't back down now. If Simon's research hinted at deeper truths about Windy Hollow, she needed to unearth them.

A short while later, the warm glow of sunrise seeped into the bakery. The scent of chai steeping on the back counter mingled with buttery croissants warming in the oven. She moved with quiet determination, prepping the space for another day—but her thoughts were already miles ahead.

The bell above the bakery door jingled. Penny entered with a paper bag and her usual air of chaotic optimism, brushing a few drops of foggy drizzle from her scarf.

"Three things," she said, holding up fingers. "Bagels, a theory, and emotional baggage. You choose."

Beth didn't smile this time. She barely looked up from her phone.

"I haven't heard from Manny," she said quietly.

Penny's smile faded. She set the bag down gently on the table.

"What's going on, Beth?"

Wordlessly, Beth turned her laptop toward Penny and showed her the ancestry research—the DNA match, the hidden Stonehurst connection.

Penny leaned in, her eyes scanning the screen. Her mouth parted slightly. Her brows lifted higher with each scroll.

Finally, she exhaled. "Of course," she murmured. "Of course! It all lines up. The teacup symbol! Oh, that's brilliant Beth! Those Stonehursts were sneaky bastards!"

Beth nodded. "If Simon found this, it's enough motive to want him gone. And if we're right—"

"Then someone's trying to control the story," Penny finished. "Or erase it completely."

Beth looked toward the window. "We need to bring this to the police."

"We are the police—well, one-third of us," Penny said. "And that third is missing."

She looked out the window. Fog still clung to the square, unmoved and uninviting.

Beth texted Manny again.
Still no response.

That afternoon, Beth and Penny were out in the fog. Snickers trotted close at their heels, his ears twitching at every unfamiliar sound.

"Nothing at the inn," Penny said, brushing mist from her sleeves. "And no one at Dusty Relics either, unless you count a very judgmental taxidermied raccoon."

Beth shook her head, glancing around the empty street. "The fog's making it worse. Feels like we're the only ones left in town."

They turned down another lane, calling Manny's name occasionally, though the sound barely carried. At the hardware store, a clerk said he hadn't seen Manny since the day before. They even swung by the town gazebo—no Manny. Just a windchime tinkling aimlessly in the gloom.

As they paused at the bakery steps, Beth rubbed her arms. "Do you think we could track his phone?"

Penny frowned. "I'm not in his Find My network. Are you?"

Beth shook her head, pulling out her phone. "Of course not."

Just then, her smartwatch buzzed.

"Ugh, it's that reminder again," she muttered. "Asking if I'm doing an outdoor walk. I swear this thing is passive-aggressive."

Penny tried to smile. "Maybe it just knows you're stress-pacing half the village."

Beth tapped it off, then stopped. Her eyes widened.

"Wait." Beth sat straighter. "The fitness app. We're all linked in that group challenge, remember?"

Penny blinked, catching on. "Yes! The step-count smackdown! Can you see where he last synced?"

Beth opened the app, scrolling through with trembling fingers. Then—

"There," she whispered. "Near the parish church. That's his last GPS ping—twenty feet from where we are right now."

Penny's voice dropped. "That's... right where the old courthouse used to be, before the fire."

Beth nodded, heart pounding. "And it's where they built the Historical Society building after. That's the Founder's Vault."

They didn't need to say more. Coats, flashlights, Snickers' leash—they were gone in less than a minute, swallowed by the thickening fog.

The streets were quiet. The fog clung low, turning familiar shapes into shadows. Beth's boots tapped lightly on damp pavement, the sound swallowed by mist. A dog barked somewhere in the distance, muffled and abrupt. No one else was out. Not even the usual jogger or the old man who fed the crows.

As they reached the church's back entrance, Snickers stopped, ears perked.

Beth found the old service door partially ajar. Just to the right of the entrance, a bronze nameplate gleamed dully through the fog. She paused to read it:

In memory of the 1912 fire that claimed the original courthouse and archives. Rebuilt with resolve and reverence. May 1915.

As she reached for the handle, she paused, her flashlight beam catching the glint of something on the ground nearby—a thin trail of dried mud. Her skin prickled. Maybe nothing—or maybe someone had been here. Not long ago.

Inside, the air was cooler. Musty. They crept down a narrow hall lit only by the beams of their flashlights.

As they stepped deeper into the church, a faint creak echoed from somewhere behind a stack of old hymnals. Snickers let out a sharp bark, startling them both.

Beth swung her flashlight toward the sound—just in time to catch a rat skittering across the far wall. She exhaled.

"Classic," she whispered. "We get a rat jump scare before the real horror show."

"Very on-brand," Penny murmured.

Beth nodded, but unease settled in her gut like a stone.

Toward the back, Beth spotted something strange: a faint glimmer outlining the edges of what looked like old floorboards—boards that didn't quite match the rest of the hall. As they stepped closer, a faint draft blew through a seam that ran down the middle.

"It's a cellar door," Penny said slowly, crouching beside it. "But it's been painted over. Maybe to keep people out... or just forgotten."

Beth ran her hand along the edge, feeling the uneven texture where the paint had cracked and flaked. "Forgotten by most people. But not everyone."

They pried at the edge, nails creaking, until the old wood groaned upward to reveal the dark cellar beneath.

Beth exhaled slowly. "If anything jumps out at us, I swear I'm baking a curse into every pie I sell."

Penny aimed her flashlight down the steps. "This isn't the Founder's Vault."

Beth nodded grimly. "No. But I think what we're looking for is beyond it."

Penny sighed. "Of course it is. Because the answer to a hundred-year-old conspiracy is never just in the first creepy basement we find."

Beth managed a faint smile. "If it ever is, I'm retiring from amateur sleuthing and opening a second bakery—one without mystery or mold."

"Or murder," Penny added, peering into the darkness. "That feels like a key ingredient to leave out."

They descended, one careful step at a time.

At the bottom, the passage opened into a stone chamber lined with shelves, crates, and cobwebbed files.

"The Founder's Vault," Beth whispered.

A dim light glowed from a crack in the far wall.

Penny found a latch hidden behind a loose stone. The wall creaked open.

There, in a small cement room, sat Manny—tied to a chair, a nasty welt on his forehead. His eyes fluttered open as they rushed forward.

Beth reached for his gag. "Manny! Are you okay?"
His eyes widened. Then he tried to shake his head.
From the shadows behind them, a voice spoke.
"You couldn't stay away, could you?"

Chapter 9

The Founders' Vault

The air in the Founders' Vault was thick—damp stone and chill curling around Beth's spine. The drip-drip-drip of water from somewhere unseen echoed through the space, each drop louder than the last in the silence that followed the voice.

"You couldn't stay away, could you?"

Beth's flashlight snapped toward the sound. Shadows scattered. Behind her, Penny gasped. Manny tried to call out, but the gag muffled his voice.

"Who's there?" Beth demanded, her voice stronger than she felt.

The figure stepped forward into the dim shaft of light.

Jack Tilley.

His coat was immaculate, even here, but the tight line of his mouth and the gun in his hand told a different story.

Beth's breath caught. "Jack."

"I warned you," he said quietly. "I told you to let this go."

Penny moved in front of Manny protectively. "You tied up a police officer, Jack."

"I did what I had to do," he said. "You think this town would understand if they knew what Simon planned to expose?"

Beth's flashlight trembled slightly in her grip. "You killed him."

"I preserved my legacy and this town," Jack snapped.

"You poisoned him," she continued, heart hammering. "But how? The toxicology couldn't find an agent."

Jack's mouth tightened. "I needed something fast. It wasn't supposed to go this far. I didn't plan for it. But when Simon started asking about the Tilley money, questioning the philanthropy... I knew where he was headed. And I knew he'd find it."

He looked past them, voice lower now. "That shed... I remembered it from my youth. The town used to store pesticides and maintenance chemicals back there. When we stopped using them, the stuff was just left behind. No paperwork. No inventory. Just dust and forgotten danger."

He took a shaky breath. "I broke in and found what I needed—a thick, cloudy bottle with no label, no markings. Just tucked behind a stack of rusted shears and bent rakes. It was old, but potent. And untraceable."

"It wasn't elegant," he muttered, exhaling shakily. "But it was untraceable. I broke in and took one of the unlabeled bottles. I set the fire to cover my tracks. The shed was already dry as kindling. When the fire took care of the rest... I thought I was in the clear."

"He was going to go public," Jack said, his voice harder now. "He confronted me right here. Asked me where the money came from—the Tilley donations, the scholarships, the restoration projects. He wanted to trace it all back. And he could. He had the tools, the DNA, the documents."

"You could've come clean," Beth said.

Jack laughed bitterly. "And what? Be the villain in a town I've spent my life trying to repair? My great-grandfather was a Stonehurst. He helped ruin this place. He bribed officials, stole land, rerouted public funds into private estates. He got away with it. But the name was filth. That's why we changed it."

Jack turned his glare on Penny. "Back away from him," he barked, motioning toward Manny with the gun. "Now."

Penny hesitated, casting a glance at Beth.

"Do it," Jack snapped.

Penny slowly stepped back from Manny, raising her hands.

Then he turned the barrel of the gun toward Beth. "Both of you—on your knees."

Beth's breath hitched. She hesitated, but one glance at Jack's shaking hand and his hard-set jaw told her this was not a bluff.

Penny and Beth lowered themselves slowly to the ground, Beth motioning for Snickers. "Stay," she whispered, her voice barely audible.

Snickers growled low, planting himself in front of her, tense and unblinking.

"Control your dog," Jack snapped, his voice cracking.

Beth's heart thundered in her ears as she gently reached out.. "It's okay, boy. Sit. Stay."

Snickers reluctantly obeyed, but didn't take his eyes off Jack.

"That's better," Jack muttered, his gaze wild now. "I didn't want it to come to this. I really didn't. My father spent his life trying to make up for what we were. And I—well, I built something better. I gave back. But Simon... Simon wouldn't leave it alone. He wanted to make a story out of it."

Beth's voice didn't waver. "So you made sure he couldn't."

"I gave him a drink. He thanked me. He smiled." Jack's voice faltered. "He didn't know. He trusted me. There was a moment... when he took the cup, I thought about stopping him. I almost did. But I told myself it was necessary. That if I let him publish, everything I'd worked for would burn." Jack's voice cracked. "I watched him die and prayed it would look natural."

Penny flinched.

Beth's jaw clenched. "And the brick?"

Jack's eyes flicked toward her. "You were getting too close."

Beth couldn't breathe for a moment. Then she took a step forward.

Her heart hammered. For a moment, she froze— really froze—because she didn't know what would happen next. He had a gun. He had rage. But then she saw Snickers, unmoving at her feet, trusting her. She straightened.

"You talk about legacy, about saving this town— but you let fear define your choices."

Beth's voice trembled—not from fear, but from the weight of memory. "My mom built a legacy here too. Not with land or plaques, but with kindness. She gave cookies to kids who got C's on spelling tests and pies to grieving neighbors. My husband? He believed you measured a man's worth by what he gave, not what he hid."

She met Jack's eyes. "You had the chance to turn your name into something meaningful. But you let the past scare you into repeating it. Simon didn't want to destroy Windy Hollow. He wanted the truth. We all do."

Jack's jaw clenched. His eyes flicked toward Beth—just for a second—when she mentioned Graham. There was something in his expression: guilt, maybe grief. A man standing in the ashes of everything he'd tried to rebuild.

"I am the truth," Jack growled. "Without me, this town doesn't stand."

Beth's fists clenched. He still didn't get it.

She thought of the villagers who'd left scones at her door when she returned, the whispered stories over pie, the history handed down in recipe cards and mismatched coffee mugs. Truth wasn't about power—it was about community. Shared memories. Honest legacies.

It wasn't always pretty, but it was real.

"No," Beth said. "It stands because of people who show up, who work, who love this place. You tried to bury the past. We're here to unearth it."

A vibration buzzed faintly in Penny's coat pocket. Jack's eyes snapped toward her, and she froze.

"Don't," he said coldly. "No one's calling anyone."

Beth's heart pounded. She had no idea if Penny's signal had gone through in this underground bunker—or if anyone would get there in time. Every second Jack talked, their window shrank.

He stepped toward Penny, eyes dark. "Back away from him," he barked, motioning toward Manny with the gun. "Now."

Penny moved slowly, hands raised, retreating from the chair where Manny sat bound. Her eyes flicked toward Beth in silent panic.

Jack turned the barrel of the gun toward Snickers. "And control that mutt before I do."

Beth's breath caught. She knelt beside Snickers and pulled him close. "It's okay," she whispered, gripping his collar firmly. "Stay with me, buddy."

Snickers gave a low growl, but stilled under her touch, his body tense.

Beth swallowed hard. "So this is your legacy then? Silencing anyone who knows the truth?"

Penny slowly lowered her hand, her phone still hidden in her coat.

Jack's expression flickered—something between recognition and regret.

"You want to talk about legacy?" Beth asked, her voice low but unwavering. "It means Simon's notes. The land grants. We have the proof. Simon's research was uploaded before he died. We found the drive and the message thread," Beth added. "The one linked to the teacup symbol in Simon's notes? I found a genealogy user—RedRoseTea1967. She's a Tilley. Marg Tilley. And she'd just discovered she shares DNA with a Stonehurst descendant named Patty. They were messaging back and forth, trying to piece together why their family trees overlapped."

Now Jack's expression darkened.

"Simon found it too, didn't he?" Penny said quietly.

"He did," Beth said. "And he tried to give you a chance to explain."

Jack's face twisted. "You don't understand—"

"I understand enough."

Jack's jaw tightened. "You think this is easy for me? You think I wanted to be here, doing this?"

Beth's voice stayed steady. "Then what's your plan, Jack? What happens after this?"

He hesitated, the muscles in his throat working. "I don't know. Maybe I disappear—find a place where no one knows the name Stonehurst. But that won't undo what's been set in motion."

He looked between them, eyes heavy. "I didn't want to kill anyone else. But if I annot preserve what I built, I will at least control the ending."

Beth clenched her fists. "So you'd destroy every bit of progress you made, just to protect a lie?"

Jack didn't answer. His grip on the gun wavered, then after a long moment, a steely determination set upon him. He steadied. And aimed.

And then—

Footsteps echoed from the staircase.

"Jack Tilley!" a voice called. "Drop the weapon!"

Manny's eyes closed in relief as Officer Jensen and two deputies appeared, flashlights slicing through the gloom.

Jack froze.

"Drop it now!"

The room held its breath.

Then he lowered the gun.

Jensen moved quickly, relieving him of the weapon while the deputies stepped in.

Beth let out a long, shaking breath. Penny rushed to untie Manny, who sagged with exhaustion but smiled weakly.

"Thanks for tracking us down! We tried to keep him speaking as long as possible."

"Typical villain monologuing - gets them every time," Penny said. "Beth, you are a bad ass!" Snickers seconded the motion with a bark.

Beth sat down on a nearby crate, heart pounding, chest tight. Her mind spun—not just from what had almost happened, but from how far they'd come. She thought of the first morning at the bakery, hands in dough, full of hope and nerves. How ridiculous her biggest fear had seemed then—naming the bakery. Now she'd stared down a murderer with her best friend and her dog by her side.

She let out a breath she didn't know she'd been holding, blinking away the sting in her eyes. "We actually did it," she whispered. "We didn't just bake pies. We cracked a case."

Snickers whined and nudged her leg. She smiled faintly, resting her hand on his head, her fingers twisting gently in his fur.

It was over.

The web was unraveling. The truth was free.

Windy Hollow could breathe again. Outside, the morning fog was finally lifting, peeling back to reveal sunlight on wet cobblestones. The storm had passed— but the truth remained, warm as cinnamon and just as lasting.

And this time, no one would sweep it back under the rug.

Chapter 10

Finished with a Flourish

The sun crested gently over Windy Hollow, spilling gold across cobblestone streets and making the bunting above the bakery shimmer like sugar-dusted frosting. A faint breeze stirred blooming lilacs along the square, mingling their scent with warm cinnamon rolls drifting from the bakery windows.

Beth stood behind the counter, her apron dusted with flour, cheeks flushed with joy. The grand opening was in full swing. Villagers bustled in and out of the shop, chatting over paper cups of chai and licking jam off their fingers. Twinkle lights crisscrossed above the bakery's entrance, and a handmade banner read: *Welcome to Sweets and Treats!*

"Sweets and Treats! Love it!" Penny smiled as she slipped behind the counter, a tray of fresh lemon bars in hand.

"It's finally official," Beth said, beaming.

Penny grinned. "And to think, you were almost stuck with 'Beth's Place'."

Beth laughed. "Don't remind me. I nearly settled because I was too scared to claim something personal. This… this feels right."

Penny sniffled theatrically. "I'm not crying, you're crying. Also, dibs on naming the first cupcake 'Alibi Almond'."

Snickers barked once in approval and promptly trotted to his honorary booth, where a sign read 'Employee of the Month: 5 Months Running'.

Manny leaned against the counter, sipping iced coffee. "I still can't believe you three cracked a murder case."

Beth grinned. "We cracked more than that. We cracked open an entire town's history."

He raised an eyebrow. 'And nearly got yourselves killed.'

Penny shrugged. 'Minor detail.'"

"I mean it," *Manny said, more serious now.* "Thank you. For getting me out. For not giving up."

Beth reached across the counter and gave his hand a squeeze. "We're a team. Always."

People continued to pour in—neighbors, old classmates, even a few out-of-towners who'd read about the story online. Ernest Mulrooney claimed he always suspected Jack Tilley. "Man had a mayor's handshake and a villain's mustache," *he declared.*

"I thought he was just well-groomed," *said Greta from the flower shop.*

"Exactly," *Ernest replied.* "Suspicious."

At one point, Mrs. Pettigrew announced, "I told my bridge club something was fishy the moment he funded that gazebo. Nobody invests in civic beautification without an agenda."

Penny leaned in. "Beth, you realize everyone is now claiming they cracked the case first?"

"I think Snickers is next," Beth said, watching the corgi accept a dog biscuit from a small child in a detective hat.

The bakery was filled with laughter, with healing. A photo of Evelyn and a small, framed newspaper clipping about Simon's last book sat near the register, surrounded by lemon bars and commemorative teacup cookies.

People shared memories of Simon—his visit, his words, his curiosity. They talked about Windy Hollow's past, not in hushed tones, but openly, with a kind of reverent honesty.

"Beth," Jay waved from the coffee station, phone in hand. 'You're trending again. Snickers's taste-test video just hit fifteen thousand views.'

"Is that the one where he tries to eat the doughnut hole and it gets stuck on his nose?" Lex added, grinning. "That's gold."

Beth laughed. "Glad my corgi is a viral sensation."

"You need to capitalize on this," Jay said. "I have TikTok ideas. One includes Snickers in a trench coat."

"And a square interrogation scene," Lex added. "Very noir. Very flaky."

Beth rolled her eyes but smiled. "Just make sure I don't have to sing."

"You could call it Crumbs & Clues: The Musical," Penny chimed in.

Beth passed around a tray of her mother's lemon sugar cookies, each one topped with a tiny swirl of frosting and a miniature teacup-shaped candy.

"Mementos of mystery?" Penny quipped.

"Legacy with a lemon zest," Beth countered.

"So," Penny said, nudging Lex. "Do we think the mayor's garden gnome mystery counts as a proper sequel?"

"Only if the gnome turns out to be a time capsule," Lex replied.

As the afternoon sun cast longer shadows across the square, Beth finally took a seat beside Manny and Penny at a table near the window.

"It feels like we turned the page on something today," she said.

Manny nodded. "We did. You did."

"As long as I don't have any more crime scenes in my store", Penny muttered.

He looked around the bakery, then back at Beth. "You didn't just build a shop, Beth. You built something that pulled this town back together."

Penny raised her glass of sparkling cider. "To Windy Hollow. Still weird. Still wonderful."

"To Beth's new bakery, Sweets and Treats," Manny added.

Beth smiled, lifting her own glass. "And to whatever story finds us next."

As conversation buzzed around her, Beth leaned back and let herself soak it in. The light. The love. The shared space that had once been a dream scribbled in her mother's recipe book.

She thought back to the first morning in the bakery. To doubting if she belonged. To wondering if her place here was real or borrowed. She used to wonder if anyone would take her seriously—a grieving widow with a rolling pin, trying to rebuild a life from scratch. But Windy Hollow had answered her in cinnamon and laughter and late-night stakeouts.

And now? Now, she had built something. Solved something. Shared something meaningful with people who mattered.

The mystery had been terrifying, yes—but also exhilarating. It had drawn out courage and connection she didn't know she had. And best of all? She'd done it with her friends.

In the corner, Snickers barked joyfully at a group of kids playing with his favorite ball.

Beth called out, "Snickers! No interrogating toddlers!"

As the celebration wound down, a hush settled over the bakery. It felt almost too quiet after the tension of the vault—like Windy Hollow itself was finally exhaling. Later, as the sun dipped below the hills, Beth stepped outside with Snickers at her side. The bakery glowed behind her. Lanterns flickered. Laughter echoed. Penny and Manny were inside helping box leftovers for the town council.

Beth looked out across the village she'd grown up in—and now, helped save. She ran her hand over the edge of the sign bearing her mother's name. A legacy restored. A future reimagined.

Snickers gave a happy yip and nudged her leg.

"I know, buddy," she whispered. "We earned this."

The air was warm. The street hushed. And Windy Hollow, bathed in amber light, was free of the weight of its secrets.

For now.

Bonus Recipe!

I hope you had a good time reading my book.

Every story will end with one of my favorite recipes. Please enjoy them with your loved ones.

Warning: *MILK, EGG, NUT, GLUTEN present*

🍁 Maple Citrus Buttertarts 🍁
- with Toasted Pecans -

- **Yields: 24 standard tarts**
- **Skill Level: Intermediate**
- **Total Time: 1 hour 15 minutes (plus chilling)**

A spirited twist on the classic Canadian buttertart. These golden pastries are filled with rich maple-caramel custard, brightened with orange zest, and finished with a toasty pecan crunch. A flaky homemade pastry keeps the gooey center perfectly contained. These are everything a buttertart should be — and then some.

🧁 Ingredients
For the Pastry Shells:
- *2½ cups all-purpose flour*

- *1 tbsp granulated sugar*
- *1 tsp salt*
- *1 cup (2 sticks) unsalted butter, cold and cubed*
- *1 large egg*
- *1 tbsp white vinegar*
- *¼ cup cold water, plus more as needed*

For the Filling:
- *1 cup packed dark brown sugar*
- *½ cup pure maple syrup*
- *½ cup unsalted butter, melted*
- *3 large eggs*
- *2 tsp vanilla extract*
- *1 tsp finely grated orange zest*
- *½ tsp flaky sea salt (or ¼ tsp fine salt)*
- *¾ cup golden raisins or chopped dried figs (optional)*
- *¾ cup toasted pecans, chopped*

Instructions
1. Make the Pastry:

In a large bowl, whisk together flour, sugar, and salt. Cut in butter using a pastry blender or fingertips until pea-sized crumbs form. In a small bowl, whisk egg, vinegar, and water. Drizzle over dry mixture, mixing gently until dough begins to clump. Turn out, knead briefly, divide in half, flatten into discs, wrap, and chill for 1 hour or overnight.

2. Prepare the Filling:

Whisk brown sugar, maple syrup, melted butter, eggs, vanilla, orange zest, and salt until smooth. Stir in raisins or figs (if using) and pecans.

3. Assemble the Tarts:

Preheat oven to 375°F. Roll chilled dough to ⅛-inch thickness. Cut into 4-inch rounds and press into 2 standard muffin tins (12 wells each). Chill the lined tins for 15 minutes. Divide filling evenly, filling each shell about ¾ full.

4. Bake:

Bake for 18–22 minutes, until pastry is golden and filling is bubbling. Cool in tins for 10 minutes, then transfer to a wire rack. The filling will set as it cools.

Tips & Twists

- **Bourbon-Laced:** *Stir 1 tbsp bourbon into the filling for a sultry depth.*
- **Mini Marvels:** *Use mini muffin tins and 3-inch rounds for bite-sized versions. Bake 14–16 minutes.*
- **Garnish with Flair:** *Top warm tarts with a pinch of flaked sea salt or a candied orange peel twist.*

Serve slightly warm with tea or tuck into a dessert platter — either way, these buttertarts bring buttery brilliance with every bite.

Enjoy!

Iris Kingsley

Printed in Dunstable, United Kingdom